DOLPHINS · LOON

TS · CANADA G

OU · PRAIRIE DOG

BINS · YOU AND ME

TS · CA GEES

DOL LOONS

OU · PRAIRIE DOG

ME · CHIMPANZEE

· DOLPHINS · LOON

RIBOU · HONEYBEE

EPHANTS · WOLVE

AND ME · ROBIN

ANIMAL FAMILIES,
ANIMAL FRIENDS

by GRETCHEN WOELFLE
illustrated by ROBERT HYNES

NORTHWORD PRESS
Chanhassen, Minnesota

The illustrations were created using acrylics on vellum bristol board
The text and display type were set in Berkeley Oldstyle and Avant Garde Gothic
Composed in the United States of America
Designed by Lois A. Rainwater
Edited by Aimee Jackson

Books for Young Readers
NorthWord Press
18705 Lake Drive East
Chanhassen, MN 55317
www.northwordpress.com

Library of Congress Cataloging-in-Publication Data

Woelfle, Gretchen.
Animal families, animal friends / by Gretchen Woelfle ; illustrated by Robert Hynes.
       p.   cm.
ISBN 1-55971-901-X (hc with dust jacket)
1. Familial behavior in animals-Juvenile literature. 2. Cooperativeness-Juvenile literature. I. Hynes, Robert, ill. II. Title.

QL761.5.W64 2004
591.5-dc22   2004002892

Printed in Singapore
10 9 8 7 6 5 4 3 2 1

To my family of writers, Alexis and Sherrill,
and to The Hive:
April, Carolyn, Cat, Dave, (another) Gretchen,
Jeanne Marie, Jo Ann, Laura, Leslie, Lindan, Marian,
Marti, Mary Ann, Meribeth, and Phyl

—G.W.

To Marc Moyens and Komei Wachi for being there

—R.H.

PEOPLE LIKE TO LIVE TOGETHER
and help each other. Our parents
make a home for us. They play
with us and teach us many things.
Grandparents, aunts, uncles, and
cousins are part of our family, too.
We make friends with our neighbors
and children at school.

Animals have parents, families,
and neighbors, just like we do. And,
like us, they often live together and
help each other.

ANIMAL PARENTS

MOTHER AND FATHER BEAVER work together to build a home for their family. They use their long teeth to chop down trees. Then they pile the trees in a stream to make a beaver lodge. The lodge is half under water and half above water. There, beaver babies live with their parents for two years. Then they find a mate, build a new lodge, and raise their own families.

EMPEROR PENGUINS LIVE in Antarctica, the coldest place on Earth. After Mother Penguin lays an egg, Father holds it on his feet and covers it with a flap of feathered skin to keep it warm. Thousands of father penguins huddle together for warmth. They stand for two months without eating or drinking until their chicks hatch. Then Mother and Father Penguin take turns keeping their chick warm and hunting for food.

MOTHER DOLPHIN feeds her baby milk. She swims beside him and tucks him under her flipper when they sleep. Father Dolphin teaches his baby how to behave. When little dolphins play too roughly, bump into grownups, or wake them up, Father claps his mouth shut to make a loud noise. He means "Stop that!" If his child does not obey, Father Dolphin nips his tail.

MOTHER AND FATHER LOON build a nest together. After Mother lays one or two eggs, Father may build extra nests to fool their enemies about where the loons live. Mother and Father take turns sitting on the eggs. After the chicks are born, both parents teach them to swim, dive, and catch fish. The baby loons ride on their parents' backs. They find a cozy seat right between the wings.

ANIMAL FAMILIES

WOLF FAMILIES live together in packs. Father is the leader and decides where to hunt, when to rest, and where to travel. Everyone in the pack—mother, father, brothers, sisters, and even adopted wolves—helps to take care of the pups. They protect the pups from danger. They hunt for food to feed them. They baby-sit for them. The older wolves let the pups chew their tails, knock them over, and nip their muzzles. This rough play helps the pups learn how to hunt.

GRANDMOTHER ELEPHANT leads her daughters and grandchildren to find food and water. Grandmother makes sure that her family behaves properly—especially the young ones. The mothers in the herd take turns baby-sitting for the calves. A nursing mother feeds any hungry baby with her milk. When aunts and cousins return from a trip, the herd welcomes them with loud trumpeting calls. They flap their ears, turn around in circles, and twist their trunks together. It is a gigantic family reunion!

CANADA GEESE travel with their relatives twice a year. In the fall they migrate south to a warmer climate where food is plentiful in winter. Dozens of young geese, parents, grandparents, aunts, uncles, and cousins fly high in the sky in a long V. They stop each night to hunt for food and rest together. When they reach their winter home, the young leave their parents and live on their own. In the spring they gather together again to fly north for the summer.

HONEYBEES LIVE IN A HIVE. The queen lays eggs, and she is the mother of all the other bees. Her hundreds of sons, called drones, do not do any work. Her thousands of daughters, called worker bees, care for the queen and the tiny bee larvae. They also build the honeycomb and keep it clean. Then they leave the hive and fly around the neighborhood collecting flower pollen and nectar to make honey for their brothers and sisters, and their mother, the queen.

ANIMAL COMMUNITIES

LARGE HERDS OF CARIBOU live in the far north. They eat small plants that grow on the tundra. Caribou live together because it is easier to find food that way. They also protect each other from wolves and bears. If the herd is attacked, the young ones gather in the middle of a circle. The strongest caribou stay at the edge, ready to fight with sharp antlers and strong hooves.

ALL DAY LONG, ROBINS FLY through the air alone, catching insects and worms to eat. But in the evening they gather together in trees by the hundreds to sing. These concerts give young robins a chance to learn the songs they will use to find a mate. When the singing lesson is over, robins go to sleep, side by side.

PRAIRIE DOG TOWNS contain many families, each living in an underground burrow. Prairie dog families greet each other with kisses and love pats. When they see danger coming, they bark to warn the whole town. They give a loud cry, and everyone scrambles home and scurries underground.

CHIMPANZEES LIVE WITH their family and friends. When one of them finds a fig tree filled with ripe fruit, the chimp will hoot and holler to invite everyone to share the feast. Chimps spend hours each day grooming each other by gently combing and cleaning each other's fur. Every night they build new sleeping nests in the trees. Mothers and babies sleep together, with friends and relatives nearby.

LIKE THE ANIMALS, we work and play together too. We have family parties on special days. We take trips with our relatives. We help our neighbors. And when the day is over and we go home again, we feel good about just being together.

photo by Christopher Gray

GRETCHEN WOELFLE is an award-winning author of picture books, short stories, and environmental nonfiction. Her first book, *The Wind at Work: An Activity Guide to Windmills*, led to her second book, *Katje the Windmill Cat*. She has also written for *Cricket, Spider,* and *Cicada* magazines and the anthology series *Stories from Where We Live*. She received an MFA in Writing for Children from Vermont College.

Gretchen's family includes one son (Cleo), one daughter (Alice), three cats (Gus, Jelly, and Little Voice), and a grand-dog (her son's dog, Mira). She loves to hike the mountains near her home in Los Angeles, California, and counts all the wildlife there as her animal friends.

If you would like to learn more about Gretchen, visit her website at: www.gretchenwoelfle.com.

ROBERT HYNES studied at the Corcoran School of Art in Washington, D.C., and earned an MFA from the University of Maryland. He has won awards from the Society of Illustrators, *Communication Arts,* and the New York Art Directors Club. Mr. Hynes has specialized in painting scenes from nature for more than twenty years. He says illustrating children's books "provides him with great freedom to create scenes that will hold the attention and fascinate the imaginations of young readers."

BEAVERS · PENGUINS
WOLVES · ELEPHAN
HONEYBEES · CARIE
CHIMPANZEES · RO
WOLVES · ELEPHAN
BEAVERS · PENGUINS
HONEYBEES · CARIE
ROBINS · YOU AND
BEAVERS · PEN
PRAIRIE DOG
CANADA GEES
CHIMPANZEES · YO